Ouch! It Stings!

Written and Illustrated by Kook JiSeung
Language Arts Consultant: Joy Cowley

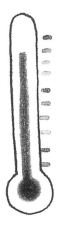

NORWOOD **H**OUSE ◆ **P**RESS
Chicago, Illinois

DEAR CAREGIVER MySELF  Bookshelf is a series of books that support children's social emotional learning. SEL has been proven to promote not only the development of self-awareness, responsibility, and positive relationships, but also academic achievement.

Current research reveals that the part of the brain that manages emotion is directly connected to the part of the brain that is used in cognitive tasks, such as: problem solving, logic, reasoning, and critical thinking—all of which are at the heart of learning.

SEL is also directly linked to what are referred to as 21st Century Skills: collaboration, communication, creativity, and critical thinking. MySELF Bookshelf offers an early start that will help children build the competencies for success in school and life.

In these delightful books, young children practice early reading skills while learning how to manage their own feelings and how to be considerate of other perspectives. Each book focuses on aspects of SEL that help children develop social competence that will benefit them in their relationships with others as well as in their school success. The charming characters in the stories model positive traits such as: responsibility, goal setting, determination, patience, and celebrating differences. At the end of each story, you will find a letter that highlights the positive traits and an activity or discussion to help your child apply SEL to his or her own life.

Above all, the most important part of the reading experience is to have fun and enjoy it!

Sincerely,

Shannon Cannon

Shannon Cannon, Ph.D.
Literacy and SEL Consultant

Norwood House Press • P.O. Box 316598 • Chicago, Illinois 60631
For more information about Norwood House Press please visit our website at www.norwoodhousepress.com or call 866-565-2900.

Shannon Cannon—Literacy and SEL Consultant
Joy Cowley—English Language Arts Consultant
Mary Lindeen—Consulting Editor

Library of Congress Cataloging-in-Publication Data
    Kook, JiSeung, author, illustrator.
    Ouch! it stings! / by Kook JiSeung ; illustrated by Kook JiSeung.
      pages cm. -- (MySELF bookshelf)
    "Social and emotional learning concepts include dealing with fear." Summary: Jun does not want to go to the doctor for a shot, and so he pretends to be a lion, too strong to need a doctor, a tortoise, too slow to get ready, and an alligator, with skin too tough to pierce, but with encouragement he learns to be brave.
    ISBN 978-1-59953-644-6 (library edition : alk. paper) -- ISBN 978-1-60357-666-6 (ebook)
    [1. Fear--Fiction. 2. Medical care--Fiction. 3. Imagination--Fiction. 4. Animals--Fiction.] I. Title.
    PZ7.K835577Ouc 2014
    [E]--dc23
                         2014009393

Manufactured in the United States of America in Stevens Point, Wisconsin.
252N—072014

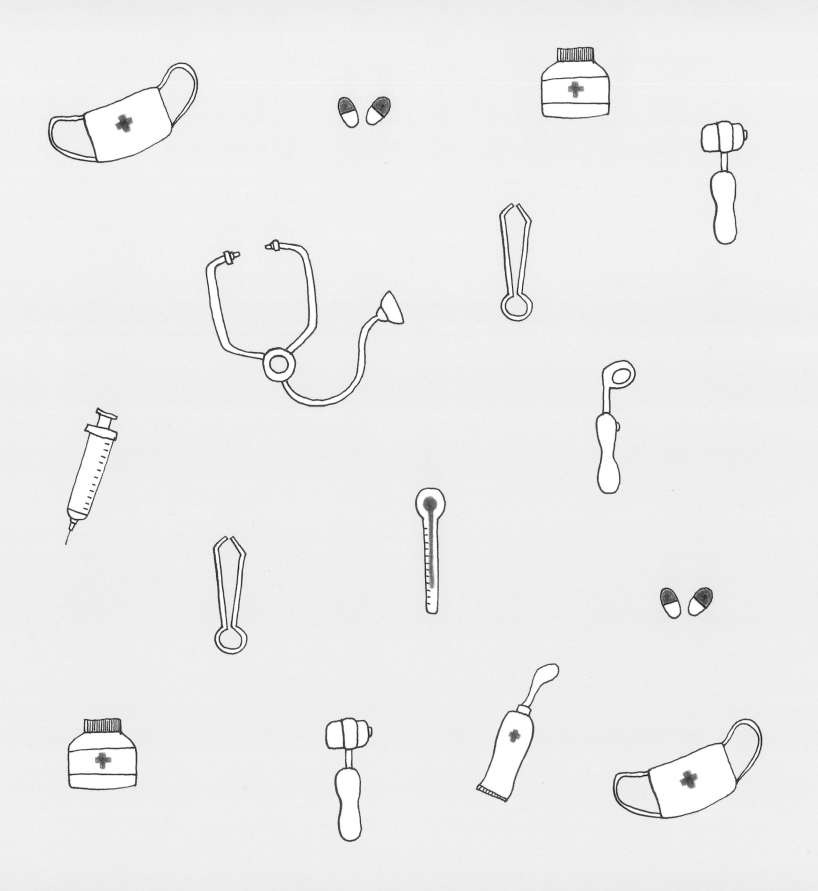

"Jun, we'll see the doctor after breakfast."

"Mom, I am not Jun."

"I am a lion!"

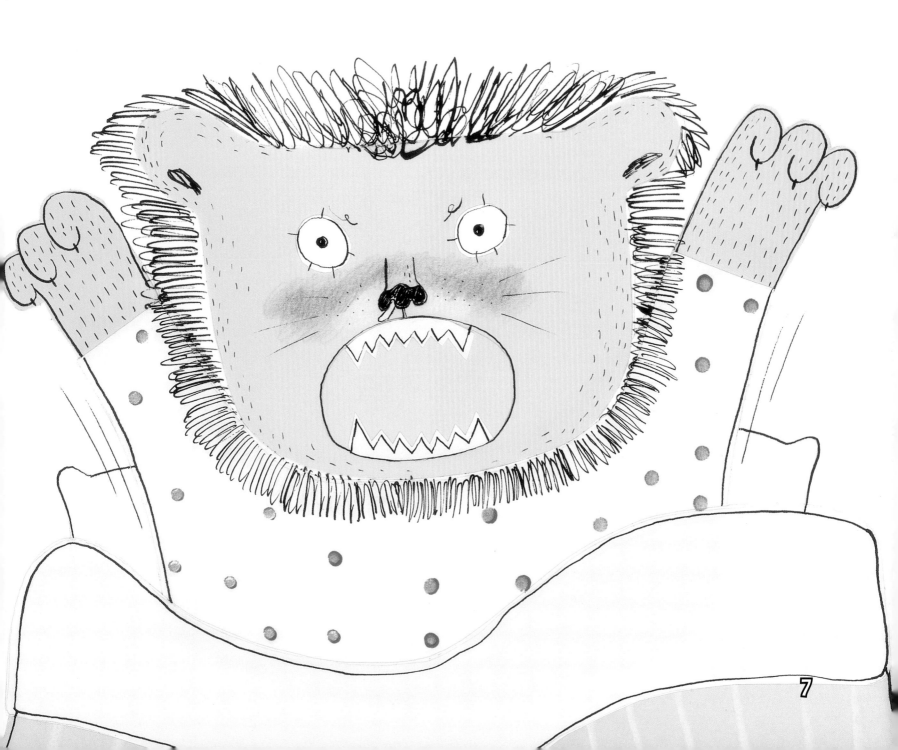

"Lions do not see the doctor.
Lions are very strong."

8

"Even lions see the doctor
when they are sick,
so they can be strong again."

"Let's get you dressed."

10

"I'm too slow to hurry, Mom.

I am a tortoise."

"Okay. We'll ride the bus."

16

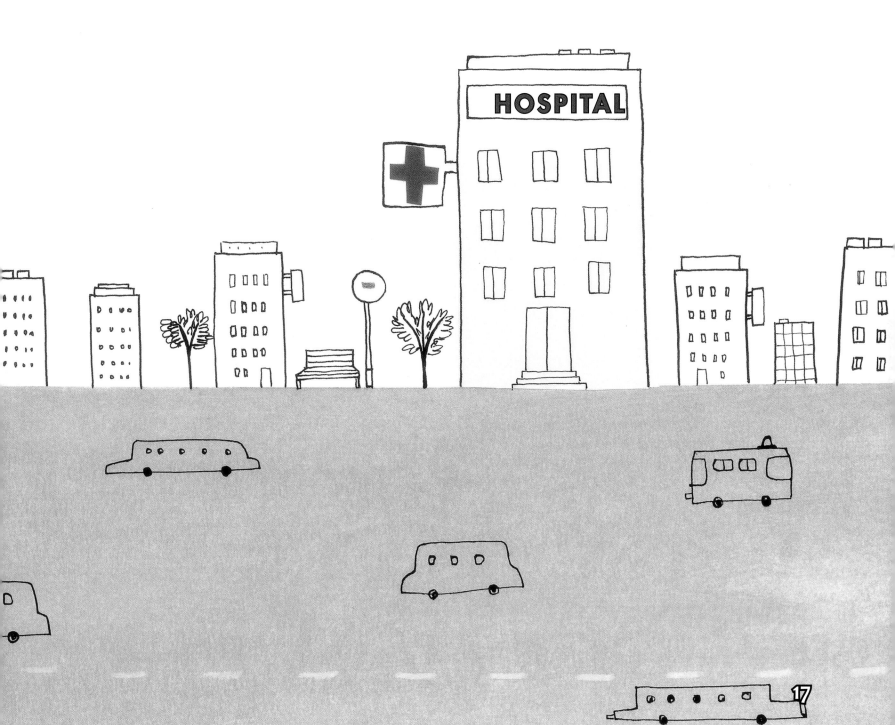

"Jun, let's sit down
and wait for the doctor."

"I am not Jun.
I am a chameleon."

"Jun, please come in!
The nurse and the doctor
are waiting."

"I am not Jun.
I am a squirrel."

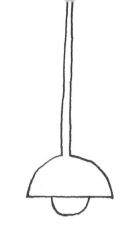

"We'll give you a shot
and you will be fine."

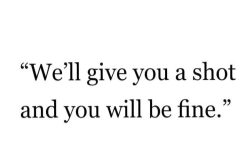

"I am not Jun.
I am an alligator!"

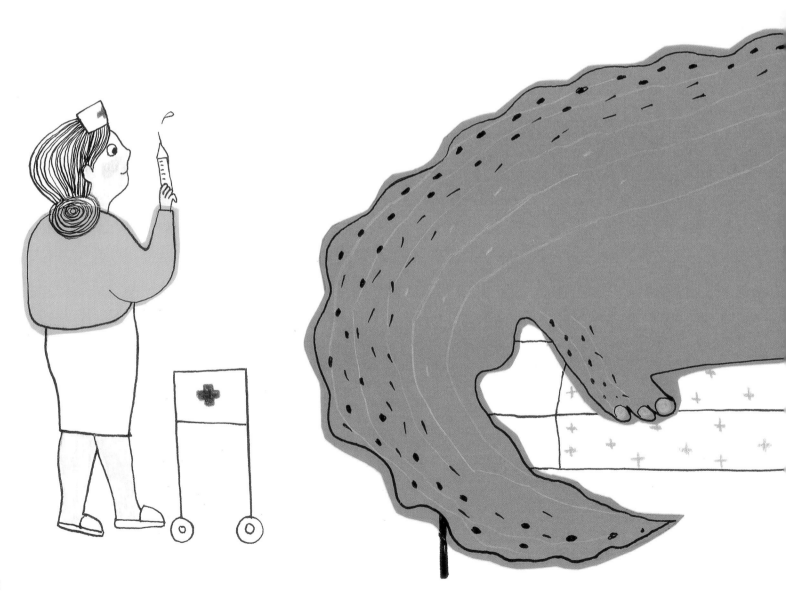

My skin is too hard for a shot.

Ouch! It stings!"

"Huh? Is that all?
It didn't hurt much."

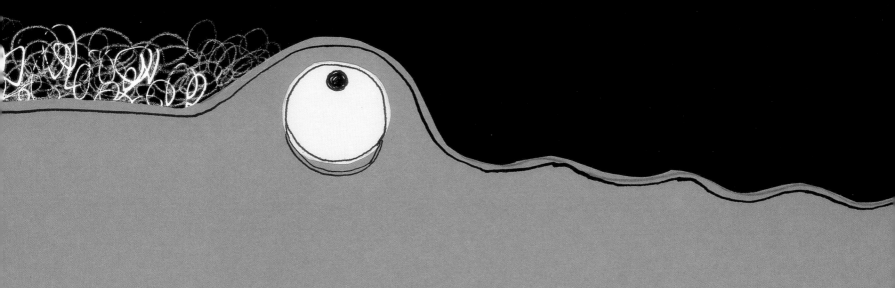

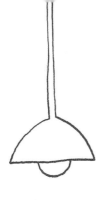

"Wow! I am very proud
of my alligator!"

28

"I am not an alligator!"

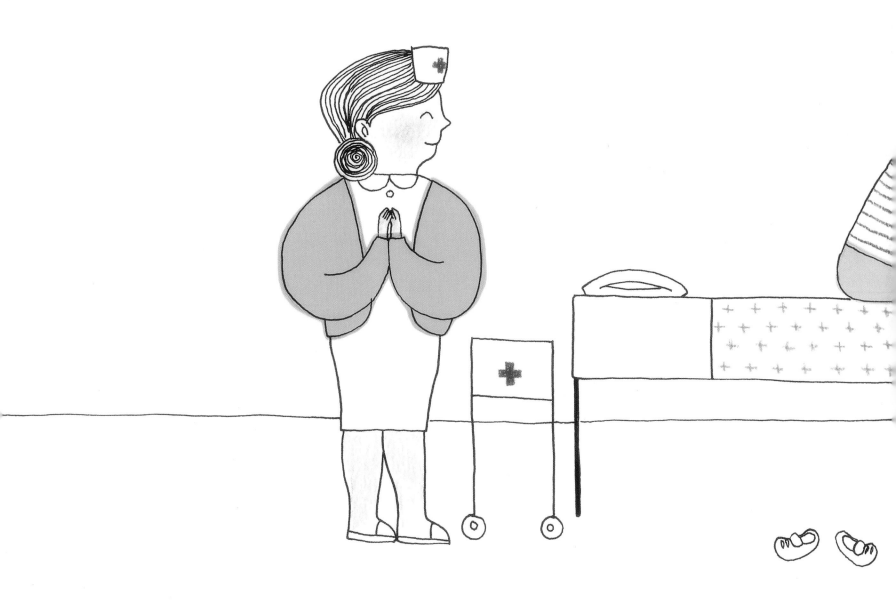

"I am brave Jun!"

Dear Jun,

I know you did not want to go to the doctor today.
It is not fun to be sick.
But, it is good to let the doctor help you
when you are sick, even if it hurts sometimes.
Today you were brave.
You let the doctor help you.
I am so proud of you!

Love, Mom

SOCIAL AND EMOTIONAL LEARNING FOCUS

Being Brave

Jun learned that sometimes we think something is going to be worse than it is, like getting a shot. He learned that being brave can make the hard things easier. On a separate piece of paper, make two columns (by folding the paper lengthwise) and list the things that you are afraid of doing or that you don't like doing. Then, next to each item, write the reason that it is important for you to do each thing. Ask your family members to create their own lists. You might be surprised at the things your caregivers do everyday, even if they don't really like to. They are brave and responsible for taking care of you, just like you are brave and responsible for the things you are supposed to do. In other words, you all know how to "take the good with the bad."

Example:

THE BAD	THE GOOD
• *Setting the table*	• *Helps my family and we get to eat together*
• *Doing homework*	• *Helps me remember what I learned in school and how to be responsible*
• *Going to bed early*	• *Rest is important for my body and will help me have a great day tomorrow*
• *Making my bed*	• *My room is neater and I start the day by being organized*
• *Can't watch TV all day*	• *Allows me to go outside and play, to use my imagination, breathe fresh air, and get exercise*

Reader's Theater

Reader's Theater is an interactive approach to reading that allows students to understand each story through dramatic interpretation. By involving students in reading, listening, and speaking activities, they provide an integrated approach for students to develop fluency and comprehension. A Reader's Theater edition of this book is available online. You can access the script by scanning the QR code to the right or visit our website at:

http://www.norwoodhousepress.com/ouch!itstings!.aspx